SUPERMAN

HEROES

THE MENACE OF METALLO

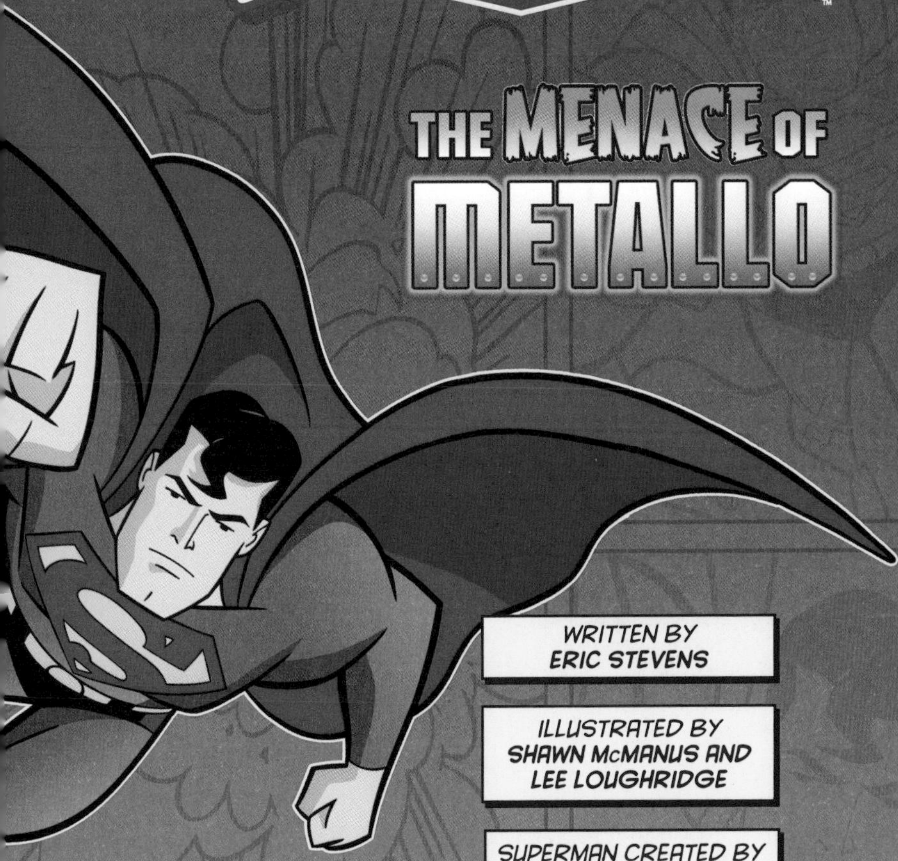

WRITTEN BY
ERIC STEVENS

ILLUSTRATED BY
SHAWN McMANUS AND
LEE LOUGHRIDGE

SUPERMAN CREATED BY
JERRY SIEGEL AND
JOE SHUSTER
BY SPECIAL ARRANGEMENT WITH
THE JERRY SIEGEL FAMILY

STONE ARCH BOOKS
a capstone imprint

Published by Stone Arch Books
A Capstone Imprint
1710 Roe Crest Drive
North Mankato, Minnesota 56003
www.capstonepub.com

STAR13229

Library of Congress Cataloging-in-Publication Data
Stevens, Eric, 1974–
   The Menace of Metallo / by Eric Stevens; illustrated by Shawn McManus.
   p. cm. — (DC Super Heroes. Superman)
   ISBN 978-1-4342-1158-3 (library binding)
   ISBN 978-1-4342-1371-6 (pbk.)
   ISBN 978-1-4342-6594-4 (ebook)
   [1. Superheroes—Fiction.] I. McManus, Shawn, ill. II. Title.
PZ7.S84443Men 2009
[Fic]—dc22   2008032441

Summary: Superman is the target of Lex Luthor's deadliest scheme. The cruel
genius has poisoned criminal John Corben. He withholds the antidote until
Corben makes a promise: he will let Luthor turn him into a robot powered
by kryptonite. But once the creature named Metallo discovers that he is more
machine than human, revenge fills his strange heart.

Adapted from the original teleplay by Stan Berkowitz.

Art Director: Bob Lentz
Designer: Bob Lentz

Printed in the United States of America
122018   001409

TABLE OF CONTENTS

CHAPTER 1

POISONED?

Off the coast of Metropolis, alone on an island in the river, sat Stryker's prison. Many have said no one could ever escape from the island. Only the most dangerous prisoners were sent to Stryker's. One of those prisoners was John Corben.

At the very end of the high-security unit, alone in his cell, Corben lay on his narrow prison bed. As always, he was thinking about Superman.

he thought.

Just then, Corben heard someone pounding on the steel door of his cell. "What now?" he said, groaning.

"I have your lunch, Mr. Corben," a shaky voice replied. It was Ralph, one of the prison's new guards.

"Come on in, Ralph," Corben said.

The heavy door creaked open. Ralph pushed in a cart with Corben's lunch. It looked more like a meal from a fancy hotel, not a prison.

"Ah," Corben said when he saw the feast. "Chicken à la king. My favorite!"

"Um, Mr. Corben, sir?" Ralph asked nervously. "How do you get such great meals in this place? Every other prisoner is eating week-old meat loaf. At least that's what it looks like!"

Corben took a bite of the soft, buttery meat and smiled. "You just need some very good friends," he said. "And always keep your mouth shut."

Corben pulled a greasy wad of cash from beneath the bed mattress. He peeled off a twenty-dollar bill and stuffed it into the guard's jacket pocket.

"Yes, sir," Ralph replied. He poured Corben a cup of coffee and headed toward the door. "Let me know if you need —"

Suddenly, Corben started coughing and gasping for air. He scratched at his neck and grabbed his chest. He tried to stand but fell, crashing into the lunch cart. Food spilled across the floor.

"Mr. Corben!" Ralph shouted. The guard quickly called for a doctor on his radio.

A few hours later, Corben awoke with a sudden breath of air. He was lying on a bed, surrounded by clean, white walls. He knew it was the prison's hospital, but didn't know how he'd gotten there.

"Mr. Corben, I'm Dr. Vale. Glad to see you're awake," said a doctor, entering the room. "The medicine must be working."

"Medicine?" said Corben, puzzled. "What's wrong with me? Why am I here?"

"You have a very rare disease," the doctor replied. "I'm afraid it's fatal."

Corben sat up in his bed, confused. "What kind of a disease?" he asked. "I take care of myself. I exercise and eat well!"

"It's a virus, Mr. Corben," the doctor answered. "Your lifestyle has nothing to do with it."

"Then I'm doomed?" Corben asked. "There's nothing you can do?!"

"Well," the doctor began. He looked down at his chart and smiled slightly. "There is an experimental treatment."

"Experimental?" Corben said, hopefully.

"It's only available from a certain good friend we both know," said the doctor. He looked over his shoulder at the nurse in the doorway. Then he leaned closer to Corben and whispered. "Lex Luthor."

Corben nearly jumped to his feet in shock. "You know my friend?" he stuttered.

"Shh," the doctor said. He placed his hand on Corben's shoulder. "Conserve your strength. You'll need it."

CHAPTER 2

ESCAPE FROM STRYKER'S

A few days later in the city of Metropolis, newspaper reporter Clark Kent enjoyed a day off from work. It was a quiet afternoon, and the sun was shining high in the sky. It was the perfect day for a bike ride. Clark decided to head out of the city, on a path near the West River.

"Ah," he sighed, coasting along the calm shoreline. "I guess it's true what they say. No news good news."

Clark continued on. Through the trees, he caught a glimpse of Stryker's Prison.

"Maybe I've finally caught them all," Clark said to himself. But even as he spoke these words, he knew they couldn't be true. Although crime in the city had dropped, it would one day return. And when it did, Clark would be there to stop it. He would stop crime as Superman, the world's most powerful hero.

Then suddenly, the quiet afternoon was shattered. Clark looked up toward the deafening roar. Two blazing missiles streaked overhead, speeding toward Stryker's Island. Dirty trails of smoke streamed behind them.

KA-BOOM! The missiles exploded into the side of the prison. A fiery cloud swirled into the sky. As the smoke cleared, Clark saw a hole in the prison's thick wall.

On Stryker's Island, criminals ran in all directions. The prison guards fired their guns into the air. They tried desperately to stop the mob of villains, but there were just too many of them.

"Let's get off this rock!" one of the prisoners shouted. He sprinted toward the hole in the security wall.

Soon, every prisoner at Stryker's had the same idea. Within minutes, the West River was full of convicts, swimming for freedom. At least they thought they were.

Clark had already shed his street clothes and changed into his Superman uniform. He soared into the air, swooped down along the river, and grabbed a giant net from a nearby fishing boat. The Man of Steel quickly scooped up most of the crooks from the water like sardines.

He dropped the net full of convicts back inside the prison. "They're all yours!" Superman said to the guards.

Superman landed and stared at the hole in the security wall. It needed fixing, and fast. Without a second thought, Superman soared into the sky. Then, like an eagle seeking its prey, the Man of Steel plunged deep into the river.

WHOOSH! Seconds later, Superman shot out of the river. He flew into the air in a geyser of water. Above his head, Superman carried a giant boulder, larger and heavier than a garbage truck.

With a mighty grunt, Superman heaved the massive rock through the air. It landed with a thud, blocking the hole in the wall and securing the prison. Unfortunately, one criminal had already managed to escape.

On the nearby shoreline, John Corben emerged from the water. He looked toward the sky and took a deep breath. "Ah, freedom!" the deadly criminal exclaimed. "I never thought I'd smell fresh air again."

Just then, a large SUV sped toward the shore. It stopped in the sand, directly in front of Corben. The driver's window quickly rolled down. Behind the tinted glass sat Dr. Vale, looking upset.

"Get in!" shouted the doctor. "We have to move!" Dr. Vale knew the police would be looking for their escaped convict. He could already hear the search helicopters.

Corben quickly hopped in the SUV. He was on a search of his own. A search to find a cure for his deadly disease.

CHAPTER 3

METALLO IS BORN

"No one's been more loyal to me than you, John," said Lex Luthor.

Luthor and a scientist stood over Corben, who lay in a hospital bed in one of the criminal mastermind's secret laboratories.

"And because of that," Luthor said, "I intend to reward you."

Luthor's scientist walked over and gave Corben an injection. "This will put you to sleep for the operation," the scientist said.

The escaped convict flinched.

"This doesn't feel like much of a reward," Corben said.

"Don't worry, John," Luthor added. "Soon you won't feel anything."

As Corben's eyes grew heavy, the scientist left the room. He soon returned, pushing in a long metal cart. On top was a mechanical skeleton.

"What's that?" Corben yelled.

"Your new lease on life," Luthor replied.

"A metal skeleton!" exclaimed Corben.

"Don't worry," Luthor added. "You'll look just as you do now."

Corben glared at his friend. "But I'll be metal on the inside," he said.

"Better than metal!" Luthor replied. "It's Metallo, and it's almost indestructible."

The scientist wheeled the cart next to Corben's bed. Corben saw a green light out of the corner of his eye.

"Is that kryptonite?" Corben asked. The drugs were making him sleepy. He couldn't even turn his head to look.

Luthor nodded. "Yes," he said. "The source of your power. It's harmless to humans, of course, but it's the only substance that can kill Superman."

Luthor looked down at Corben. "You want that, don't you?" he asked. "After all, Superman is the one who put you in jail."

Corben sighed. "What do I have to lose?" he said. Then he closed his eyes.

"Indeed," Luthor replied. But Corben was already asleep. The operation was about to begin.

Meanwhile, across Metropolis at the headquarters of the , Lois Lane and Clark Kent were watching the evening news. The top story was the breakout at Stryker's Island Prison.

"Luckily, Superman was nearby," said the news anchor. "All the prisoners were back in their cells within minutes."

The screen switched from an image of the prison to an image of John Corben. "Only one prisoner escaped," the anchor said. "John Corben."

The TV showed footage of Corben wearing a high-tech mechanical suit and fighting Superman. "Several months ago," the anchor continued, "John Corben stole the Lexosuit. This powerful suit of armor was developed by LexCorp, Lex Luthor's weapons manufacturing company."

"After an intense battle, Superman captured Corben and sent him to Stryker's Island," the anchor said. "The police are now looking into any connection between the missile attack on the prison and John Corben's escape."

Lois turned off the TV. "I'd like to know who has access to air-to-surface missiles!" she said.

Clark shrugged. "Nowadays, just about anyone," he said.

"However Corben escaped, he won't be free for long," said Lois. "Take a look at this." She handed Clark a blue folder.

"Corben's medical record?" Clark said. "How did you get this?"

"A friend at Stryker's," Lois replied. "The point is, Corben has Erosco's retrovirus."

"The rare South American disease?" Clark said. "It's one hundred percent fatal!"

"That's right," Lois replied. "So Corben's days are numbered."

"How do you suppose he got such a rare disease?" Clark asked. "It only affects people who live on a tiny island off the coast of Brazil."

Lois shrugged. "A guy like Corben?" she said. "He's been on the run from the law so many times, I wouldn't be surprised if he's been there."

•   •   •

Back at Luthor's secret laboratory, Corben's operation had ended. Corben stood next to the hospital bed. He flexed and stretched his new limbs.

"Well, how do you feel?" Luthor asked.

"Amazing," he said. "I haven't felt this good in weeks!"

"Let's test that," Luthor said. "This way." The billionaire led his new and improved friend to a large machine.

The scientist stood beside it. "This computer will measure your strength," he said. "Punch here, please." The scientist pointed to a pad on the machine.

Corben wound up and smashed his fist into the pad. The scientist checked the computer. "Impressive," he said.

"Hm," Corben said with a smirk. "I wasn't even trying. Watch this."

Again, Corben drew back his arm. This time, he punched the pad with all his strength. SMASH! The machine shattered to the floor in a heap of metal and glass.

"Satisfied, Lex?" Corben said.

"Not just yet," Luthor replied. He pointed to the other end of the lab. "Please stand over there."

Corben obeyed and stood on a red circle on the far end of the room. Suddenly, a hatch opened in the wall, and a missile came blasting toward Corben.

"Hey, wait a minute!" Corben shouted, but it was too late.

KA-BOOM! The missile struck his chest, exploding in a giant ball of fire.

After a moment, the smoke cleared. Corben stood among the shards of the destroyed missile. "Amazing," he said, looking himself over. "Not a scratch."

"Even your skin is made of Metallo," said Luthor. "Nothing can hurt you."

"But . . . I can't feel anything at all," Corben replied. "It's like I'm controlling my body from the outside. Like I'm some kind of remote control toy!"

"Well, some adjustments need to be made, that's all," Luthor said. "But first, you have a job to do."

"Superman?" Corben asked.

"Yes," Luthor said. He glanced at his gold watch. "I have a lunch to attend. I expect to hear the news of Superman's destruction by dessert."

In minutes, Corben was out on the streets of Metropolis. He walked quickly through a busy train station, planning his attack on Superman.

"Roses!" a woman called from her flower cart. "Sir, wouldn't you like to buy a rose?"

"No thanks," Corben replied.

"One rose," the woman went on, "for that special lady. They smell wonderful." She held a rose under Corben's nose.

Corben sniffed. "I can't smell anything!" he yelled. Corben pushed the woman away, and she fell to the pavement.

Now angry, Corben strode over to the tracks. Hundreds of citizens of Metropolis stood there, waiting for their train. Corben pushed through the crowd and jumped onto the tracks.

The crowd began screaming. "Look at that nut!" a man called out. "Get off the tracks!" a woman cried.

Corben only smiled as a speeding train approached. The engineer tried to stop in time, but it was no use.

Like a defensive lineman, Corben crouched and used his shoulder to stop the fifty-ton train.

The train collapsed as it struck him, as if it were a flimsy soda can.

Corben laughed and lifted a train car over his head. He cried out through his laughter, "Last stop for this train!"

An attack like this would be quickly noticed by the Man of Steel, though. In minutes, Superman was diving from above. Like a speeding bullet, he collided with Corben. At the same time, Superman grabbed the train car and placed it safely on the ground.

"I was expecting you, Superman," Corben said, still laughing.

"You're going back to jail," Superman said.

The Man of Steel grabbed Corben and tried to hold him, but Corben fought back. "I'm as strong as you now," he said. "You can't stop me! Jealous?"

"Not quite," Superman said, wrestling Corben to the ground.

"Still think it's funny, Corben?" Superman asked.

Corben laughed. "Yes," he replied. "Because you don't know my secret weapon."

Suddenly, a small panel on Corben's chest snapped open. A green light shined out. Inside his chest was a chunk of kryptonite, the only substance that could stop the Man of Steel!

CHAPTER 4

KILLER HEART

"Ha!" Corben said. "Everything okay? You're looking a bit green, Superman."

Corben wound up and punched Superman, pushing him backward onto the nearby highway. Corben jumped down after him, landing with a great crash.

"You are jealous, aren't you?" Corben said. "Now I'm the Man of Steel!"

Corben picked up a piece of concrete. He held it over his head, ready to strike the final blow on his enemy.

"You sent me to prison, Superman," he said. "Now it's payback time!"

Just then, a car screeched to a halt between them. Lois Lane threw the door open and reached out to Superman from the driver's seat. "Get in!" she cried out.

Superman was too weak to move. He moaned, struggling to get up.

Corben grabbed Lois. He pulled her from the car. "He's not going anywhere, Miss Lane," he growled.

"Don't touch me, Corben!" Lois snapped.

"Oh, you remember my name," Corben said, smiling.

He pulled her to him and roughly kissed her. Just as quickly, he released her and touched his fingers to his lips. "I . . . I didn't feel that kiss," Corben said.

"Feel this!" Lois replied, slapping Corben's face. Lois grabbed her hand and cringed in pain.

Meanwhile, Superman had struggled to his feet. He quickly climbed into Lois's car and started the engine.

"I can't even feel a kiss," Corben muttered. "What have they done to me?"

Still confused, Corben didn't notice Superman shift the car into drive and floor it. The car struck Corben head on, and sent him off the overpass.

WHAM! Corben landed on a speeding truck, away from Lois and Superman.

"Superman!" Lois said, rushing to his side. "What happened to John Corben?"

"Something wrong," Superman replied. "Something terribly wrong."

A short time later, Corben stormed into Luthor's lab and found the scientist who had done the operation.

"You!" he screamed, kicking over the scientist's desk. "I still can't feel anything! Give me the adjustments!"

"The adjustments were yours to make, Mr. Corben," the scientist replied nervously. "There will always be a certain lack of feeling. But you'll get used to it."

"I don't want to get used to it!" Corben shouted, walking toward a mirror. "It's all fake. A fraud. I am only metal behind the man, not really a man at all."

Corben clawed at his face, peeling away half of his new Metallo skin. "This is who I am now," he said. "I am the machine. I am Metallo!"

At Stryker's prison, Lois and Clark were trying to meet with Dr. Vale, the prison doctor who knew Corben. A younger doctor met them at the front gate.

"I'm sorry," he said. "Dr. Vale no longer works here."

"What a surprise," Clark whispered.

Lois ignored Clark's comment. "Could we take a look around his old office?" she asked the doctor.

"Afraid not," he said. "I've been given orders not to let anyone inside. Now if you'll excuse me, I have a patient waiting."

As the doctor walked away, Clark grabbed Lois's arm. He pulled her toward Dr. Vale's office. The door was locked, but he didn't tell Lois. Instead, Clark secretly melted the deadbolt with his heat-vision.

Once inside, Clark quickly walked over to Dr. Vale's desk. He opened a plastic box with a danger symbol on it. "It's a sharp box," Clark said. "It's for used razors, needles, and any medical garbage that might be dangerous."

"Lovely," Lois replied. She picked up a basket and started digging through it.

Meanwhile, Clark opened the sharp box. Among the used needles, he spotted a small glass tube inside. "Hmm," he muttered to himself. He grabbed the tube and placed it in his pocket.

"Look at this," Lois said. She held up a small piece of paper. "Parking validation."

"So?" Clark asked.

"It's from LexCorp," Lois replied.

CHAPTER 5

A NEW ENEMY

Along the docks of Metropolis, Lex Luthor enjoyed a sunny afternoon on the deck of his yacht. With a fruity drink in one hand and caviar in the other, he was enjoying his riches.

"How's the caviar?" came a voice from the shadows. "Does it melt in your mouth?"

"John?" Luthor said.

"Call me Metallo," Corben said. He stepped into the sunlight. He was like a walking skeleton, made of metal.

"I hope you like my new look," Corben added. "It will be the last thing you see."

Luthor stood up. "Is there a problem, John?" he said.

Corben grabbed Luthor by the collar. "Yes, there's a problem," he replied. "I can't feel anything! I can't taste or smell anything!"

"Did you think I would leave you like this?" Luthor replied. "It isn't permanent."

"Liar!" Corben snapped, dropping Luthor back into his chair. "Your scientist told me there was nothing he could do."

"Not now, Corben," Luthor said, "but someday. I have labs all over the world working on this problem. You must be patient." Corben didn't know what to believe.

Luthor got to his feet. "Get below," he ordered. "I have a lab not far from shore where we can repair your skin."

Soon, the yacht was cruising through the ocean waters toward Luthor's lab. "Don't forget, John," Luthor said as he steered the ship. "You still owe me Superman."

"Patience," Corben replied. "That's something we both need, isn't it?"

Luthor glanced up from his pilot's seat. "Hmm, maybe not," he said. "Look!"

Corben got to his feet and looked up. Superman was soaring high over the yacht but diving fast.

"Stay here," Luthor said. He headed for the deck.

Superman landed on the deck of the yacht just as Luthor left the cabin.

"Where's Corben?" Superman demanded.

"Who?" said Luthor, smiling.

"I know all about Dr. Vale," Superman said. "It's just a matter of time before the police find him."

"What makes you think there is anything left of him to find?" Luthor replied.

Just then, Corben appeared. He dived at the Man of Steel, knocking him to the lower decks of the ship.

"Corben!" Superman said, struggling to his feet. "You have to listen to me."

Corben opened the panel on his chest, revealing the kryptonite inside. Superman fell to the floor. "Corben," he struggled to speak, "you're being tricked!"

The metal man wound up and dove again at the Man of Steel. They both crashed through deck after deck, finally landing in the engine room in the belly of the ship.

"I'm not your enemy, Corben," Superman said with a gasp. "Luthor is. He did this to you."

Corben lifted Superman by his collar. "Luthor saved me from that virus," he said. "Otherwise, I'd be dead now."

Superman reached into his belt. He pulled out the tube from Dr. Vale's office.

"Here's your virus," he said. "Dr. Vale at Stryker's was putting it in your food. How did you think you got such a rare disease?"

Corben grabbed the tube. "But why?" he asked.

"Luthor told him to," Superman replied. "He paid the doctor well."

Corben screamed. With a great leap, he was back up on deck. He towered over a frightened Luthor.

"Superman is lying," Luthor said. "Don't you see? He's trying to save himself!"

"Let's see if he's lying or not," Corben said. "Here." Metallo opened the glass tube and tried to pour it into Luthor's mouth. "Drink up, Lex," he said.

Luthor struggled to keep his mouth closed.

Meanwhile, below in the engine room, Superman's powers were returning. He looked around and spotted a few tanks of fuel. With his heat-vision, he stared down at the tanks.

KA-BOOM! The tanks exploded into flames. The yacht blew to pieces, sending Corben and Luthor into the sea.

"Help!" Corben cried out. "I'm too heavy to float!" The metal man sank quickly to the ocean floor.

Luthor grabbed a floating piece of wood. A moment later, Superman scooped him from the water and carried him to the shore of Metropolis.

"You'll never pin this on me," Luthor snapped. "The virus is destroyed, and Corben is at the bottom of the sea. Even if you find him, there's still the kryptonite to worry about."

"You did this to him, Lex, and he knows that," Superman replied. "So I don't think I'm the one who should be worrying."

With that, Superman flew off, leaving Luthor to worry about Corben's revenge.

Meanwhile, at the bottom of the sea, Metallo, with no need for air to breathe, walked along the sand. Slowly, he walked back toward Metropolis and his new enemy, Lex Luthor.

DAILY PLANET

FROM THE DESK OF CLARK KENT

WHO IS METALLO?

A hardened criminal, John Corben was once employed by Lex Luthor. While imprisoned, Luthor infected Corben with a deadly virus and then offered to "save" Corben by having him undergo a medical procedure. Upon awakening, Corben felt unimaginably strong. Unfortunately, his brain had been transplanted into a cyborg body, making him a shell of his former self. Unable to feel anything but the cold embrace of metal, Corben has developed an evil side, making him a major threat to all of Metropolis.

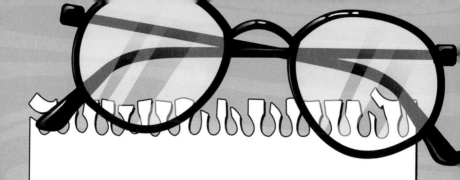

- Metallo's heart is made of pure kryptonite, which powers his exoskeleton. Without the alien mineral, Corben's cyborg body would be completely powerless.

- When the man of metal clashes with the Man of Steel, sparks really start to fly! Metallo is capable of stunning Superman with his powerful cyborg punches. By opening his chest-plate, Metallo can bathe Superman in kryptonite's lethal radiation.

- Corben was simply a pawn in Luthor's attempt to create a super-villain capable of defeating Superman. Upon discovering the truth, Metallo swore to destroy Luthor for transforming him into a metallic monster.

- Corben has grown used to his metal body, giving him the ability to transform any machinery around him into part of his own exoskeleton!

BIOGRAPHIES

Eric Stevens lives in St. Paul, Minnesota. He is studying to become a middle-school English teacher. Some of his favorite things include pizza, playing video games, watching cooking shows on TV, riding his bike, and trying new restaurants. Some of his least favorite things include olives and shoveling snow.

Shawn McManus has been drawing pictures ever since he was able to hold a pencil in his tiny little hand. Since then, he has illustrated comic books including Sandman, Batman, Dr. Fate, Spider-Man, and many others. Shawn has also done work for film, animation, and online entertainment. He lives in New England.

Lee Loughridge has been working in comics for more than 14 years. He currently resides in sunny California in a tent on the beach.

GLOSSARY

caviar (KAV-ee-ahr)—an expensive appetizer made from fish eggs

conserve (kuhn-SERV)—to save something from loss or decay, or to preserve for later use

doomed (DOOMD)—destined to fail

indestructible (in-di-STRUHK-tuh-buhl)—unable to be destroyed

injection (in-JEK-shuhn)—liquid inserted into the body for medical purposes

mastermind (MASS-ter-minde)—a person who created a specific idea or plan

shard (SHAHRD)—a piece or fragment of something larger

shattered (SHAT-erd)—broke into tiny pieces

tinted (TINT-id)—gave slight color to, or altered the color of

villains (VIL-uhnz)—wicked or evil people

DISCUSSION QUESTIONS

1. Metallo is angry because Lex Luthor made him a monster. Does this excuse his evil behavior? Explain your answer.

2. At the end of the story, Metallo is still alive at the bottom of the ocean. When he makes it to shore, what do you think he will do? Why?

3. Clark Kent's secret identity is Superman. Why do you think he keeps his alter ego a secret from everyone? Would you tell anybody if you were a super hero?

WRITING PROMPTS

1. Imagine you were changed into a robot. What material would you want to be made from? What superpowers would you want?

2. Write your own story about Superman and Metallo. How will Superman capture him? You decide.

3. Lex Luthor is a billionaire who uses his money for evil. If you were a billionaire, how would you spend your money?

MORE NEW SUPERMAN ADVENTURES!

LAST SON OF KRYPTON

THE MUSEUM MONSTERS

THE STOLEN SUPERPOWERS

TOYS OF TERROR

UNDER THE RED SUN